I CAN READ IT ALL BY MYSELF

Beginner Books

For
Lee Groo,
the Enunciator

Oh say can you Say?

By

Dr. Seuss

BEGINNER BOOKS
A Division of Random House, Inc.

6401920

Library of Congress Cataloging in Publication Data

Seuss, Dr. Oh say can you say? SUMMARY: A collection of nonsensical tongue twisters. 1. Tongue twisters. [1. Tongue twisters] I. Title.   PN6371.5.S44   428'.1   78-20716   ISBN 0-394-84255-3 (trade); 0-394-94255-8 (lib. bdg.)

Manufactured in the United States of America

Said a book-reading parrot named Hooey,
"The words in this book are all phooey.
When you say them, your lips
will make slips and back flips
and your tongue may end up in Saint Looey!"

Do you like fresh fish?

It's just fine at Finney's Diner.

Finney also has some fresher fish

that's fresher and much finer.

But his best fish is his freshest fish

and Finney says with pride,

"The finest fish at Finney's

is my freshest fish, French-fried!"

SO . . .

don't order the fresh

or the fresher fish.

At Finney's, if you're wise,

you'll say,

"Fetch me the finest

French-fried freshest

fish that Finney fries!"

Dinn's Shin

We have a dinosaur named Dinn.
Dinn's thin. Dinn doesn't have much skin.
And the bones fall out
of his left front shin.

Then we have to call in Pinner Blinn,
who comes with his handy shin-pin bin
and with a thin Blinn shinbone pin,
Blinn pins Dinn's shinbones right back in.

Bed Spreaders spread spreads on beds.

Bread Spreaders spread butters on breads.

And that Bed Spreader better

watch out how he's spreading . . .

or that Bread Spreader's
sure going to butter his bedding.

Ape Cakes
Grape Cakes

As he gobbled the cakes on his plate,
the greedy ape said as he ate,
"The greener green grapes are,
the keener keen apes are
to gobble green grape cakes.
They're GREAT!"

Are you having trouble
in saying this stuff?
It's really quite easy for me.
I just look in my mirror
and see what I say,
and then I just say what I see.

Now let's talk about MONEY!

You should leave your Grox home
when you travel by air.
If you take him along,
they charge double the fare.
And your Grox must be packed
and locked up in a Grox Box,
which costs much, much more
than a little old fox box.
So it's heaps a lot cheaper
to fly with your foxes
than waste all that money
on boxes for Groxes.

And, what do you think costs more? . . .

A Simple Thimble

or

a Single Shingle?

A simple thimble <u>could</u> cost less
than a single shingle would, I guess.
So I think that the single shingle <u>should</u>
cost more than the simple thimble would.

If you like to eat potato chips

and chew pork chops on clipper ships,

I suggest that you chew

a few chips and a chop

at Skipper Zipp's Clipper Ship Chip Chop Shop.

And if your tongue
is getting queasy,
don't give up.
The next one's EASY!

There are so many things
that you really should know.
And that's why I'm bothering
telling you so.
You should know the first names
of the Fuddnuddler Brothers
who like to pile each on the heads of the others.
If you start at the top,
there are Bipper and Bud
and Skipper and Jipper
and Jeffrey and Jud,
Horatio, Horace and Hendrix and Hud,
and then come Dinwoodie and Dinty and Dud,
also Fitzsimmon and Frederick and Fud,
and Slinkey and Stinkey and Stuart and Stud.
And, down at the bottom
is poor little Lud.
But if Lud ever sneezes,
his name will be MUD.

We have two ducks. One blue. One black.
And when our blue duck goes "Quack-quack"
our black duck quickly quack-quacks back.
The quacks Blue quacks make her quite a quacker
but Black is a quicker quacker-backer.

AND . . . speaking of quacks
reminds me of cracks
and stacks and sacks
and shacks and Schnacks.
SO . . . oh say can you say,
"I have cracks in my shack,
I have smoke in my stack,
and I think there's a Schnack
in the sack on my back!"

WEST BEAST

Upon an island hard to reach,
the East Beast sits upon his beach.
Upon the west beach sits the West Beast.
Each beach beast thinks he's the best beast.

Which beast is best? . . . Well, I thought at first
that the East was best and the West was worst.
Then I looked again from the west to the east
and I liked the beast on the east beach least.

Pete Pats Pigs

Pete Briggs pats pigs.

Briggs pats pink pigs.

Briggs pats big pigs.

(Don't ask me why. It doesn't matter.)

Pete Briggs is a pink pig, big pig patter.

Pete Briggs pats his big pink pigs all day.

(Don't ask me why. I cannot say.)

Then Pete puts his patted pigs away

in his Pete Briggs' Pink Pigs Big Pigs Pigpen.

Fritz needs Fred and Fred needs Fritz.

Fritz feeds Fred and Fred feeds Fritz.

Fred feeds Fritz with ritzy Fred food.

Fritz feeds Fred with ritzy Fritz food.

And Fritz, when fed, has often said,

"I'm a Fred-fed Fritz.

Fred's a Fritz-fed Fred."

How to tell a Klotz from a Glotz

Well, the Glotz, you will notice,
has lots of black spots.
The Klotz is quite different
with lots of black dots.
But the big problem is
that the spots on a Glotz
are about the same size
as the dots on a Klotz.
So you first have to spot
who the one with the dots is.
Then it's easy to tell
who the Klotz or the Glotz is.

What would you rather be when you Grow Up?

A cop in a cop's cap?

Or a cupcake cook

in a cupcake cook's cap?

Or a fat flapjack flapper

in a flat flapped-jack cap?

OR . . .
if you think
you don't like cops' caps,
flapjack flappers'
or cupcake cooks' caps,
maybe you're one
of those choosy chaps
who likes kooky captains' caps
perhaps.

Well, when Blinn comes home tired
from his work pinning shins,
the happiest hour of old Blinn's day begins.
Mr. Blinn is the father of musical twins
who, tucking twin instruments under twin chins,
lull their daddy to sleep with twin Blinn violins.

AND . . . oh say can you say,

"Far away in Berlin

a musical urchin named Gretchen von Schwinn

has a blue-footed, true-footed,

trick-fingered, slick-fingered,

six-fingered, six-stringed tin Schwinn mandolin."

Rope Soap
Hoop Soap

If you hope

to wash soup off a rope,

simply scrub it with **SKROPE**!

Skrope is so strong that no rope is too long!

But if you should wish to wash
soup off a hoop, I suggest that it's best
to let your whole silly souped-up hoop soak
in Soapy Cooper's Super Soup-Off-Hoops Soak Suds.

One year we had a Christmas brunch
with Merry Christmas Mush to munch.
But I don't think you'd care for such.
We didn't like to munch mush much.

And, speaking of Christmas...

Here are
some Great Gifts
to give to your daddy!

If your daddy's name is Jim
and if Jim swims and if Jim's slim,
the perfect Christmas gift for him
is a set of Slim Jim Swim Fins.

But if your daddy's name is Dwight
and he likes to look at birds at night,
the gift for Dwight that might be right
is a Bright Dwight Bird-Flight
Night-Sight Light.

But Never Give Your Daddy a Walrus

A walrus with whiskers
is not a good pet.
And a walrus which whispers
is worse even yet.
When a walrus lisps whispers
through tough rough wet whiskers,
your poor daddy's ear
will get blispers and bliskers.

And that's almost enough
of such stuff for one day.
One more and you're finished.
Oh say can you say?...

"The storm starts
when the drops start dropping.
When the drops stop dropping
then the storm starts stopping."

P.S.

And, just in case you missed it,
do not miss it any longer.
Dr. Seuss's FOX IN SOCKS*
makes twisted tongues much stronger.

*"Let the beginner read and recite with
sly Fox the simple words which always
accumulate into audible pandemonium. It
will be a riotous workout."*
—the New York Times Book Review

"It is wild and really funny."
—the Chicago Tribune

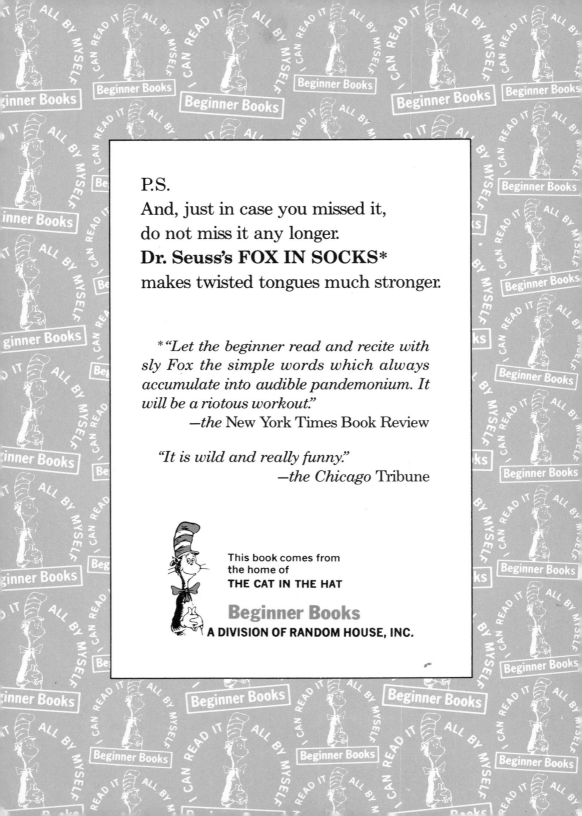

This book comes from
the home of
THE CAT IN THE HAT

Beginner Books
A DIVISION OF RANDOM HOUSE, INC.